For all the glamorous *Glam*-MAS out there, and for mine.
You GO, girls. — S.B.

For all the *Glam*-MAS we know, love,

and are inspired by. — S.R.

Text copyright © 2019 by Samantha Berger • Illustrations copyright © 2019 by Sujean Rim
All rights reserved. Published by Orchard Books, an imprint of Scholastic Inc., *Publishers since 1920.* ORCHARD BOOKS and design are registered trademarks of Watts Publishing Group, Ltd., used under license. SCHOLASTIC and associated logos are trademarks and/or registered trademarks of Scholastic Inc. • The publisher does not have any control over and does not assume any responsibility for author or third-party websites or their content. • No part of this publication may be reproduced, stored in a retrieval system, or transmitted in any form or by any means, electronic, mechanical, photocopying, recording, or otherwise, without written permission of the publisher. For information regarding permission, write to Scholastic Inc., Attention: Permissions Department, 557 Broadway, New York, NY 10012. • This book is a work of fiction. Names, characters, places, and incidents are either the product of the author's imagination or are used fictitiously, and any resemblance to actual persons, living or dead, business establishments, events, or locales is entirely coincidental.
Library of Congress Cataloging-in-Publication Data available
ISBN 978-1-338-15183-1
10 9 8 7 6 5 4 3 2 1   19 20 21 22 23
Printed in Malaysia 108 • First edition, September 2019 • Book design by Jess Tice-Gilbert

I LOVE MY
Glam♥MA

by
Samantha Berger

illustrated by
Sujean Rim

ORCHARD BOOKS ♡ NEW YORK
An Imprint of Scholastic Inc.

Everyone knows grandmothers go by many names:

Grandma

Granny

Gigi

Mom-Mom

Yaya

Meemaw

Nana

Bubbe

Abuela

Gram

Oma

Big Mama G.

But MAYBE they should really be called "*Glam*-MA."
Because Grandmas are some of the most
glamorous people you're ever gonna meet.

Glam-MAS don't just come over . . .

they make a *grand entrance!*

Glam-MAS don't just celebrate holidays . . .

WORLD'S BEST PONYTAIL MAKER

they celebrate *everything!*

Glam-MAS don't just carry a purse . . .

they carry a *treasure chest!*

Glam-MAS ask, "Why just get dressed when you can make a *statement*?"

And then *they do*!

Some *Glam*-MAS stroll . . .

and some *Glam*-MAS roll.

Some *Glam*-MAS siesta . . .

and some *Glam*-MAS fiesta.

Some *Glam*-MAS rock . . .

and some *Glam*-MAS rock OUT.

If you give a *Glam*-MA yarn,
she could knit a scarf . . .

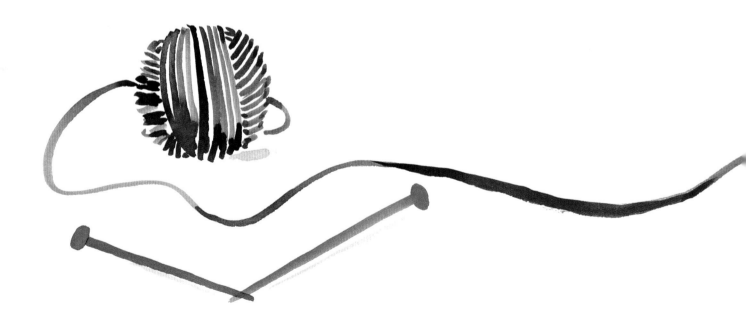

or she could knit a black belt.

If you get a *Glam*-MA a blanket,
she might make a reading fort . . .

or she might turn it into a super cape.

If you take a *Glam*-MA on vacation,
she might build a world-class sandcastle . . .

or she might go diving with dolphins.
(Possibly both!)

Glam-MAS don't follow recipes.
They follow their instincts . . .

and let YOU follow yours.

Glam-MAS don't just sing bedtime songs.
They lead the whole choir . . .
and let YOU sing the big solo.

Glam-MAS don't just throw parties.
They host the event of the season . . .

and make YOU the guest of honor.

But what is it that *really* makes a
Glam-MA so glamorous?

BEST IN LAP

NAP EXPERT

#1 STORYTELLER

WORLD'S Greatest

People's Choice

BATH GIVER

BACK-scratcher #1

Favorite CARD player

GOLD MEDAL Laugher

PERFECT ATTENDANCE RECORD HOLDER

TOP LISTENER

YOU.

Because you're the one who made her
a *Glam*-MA in the first place . . .

and nothing is more *glamorous* than that.